APPLES ~~NOT~~ & ORPLES

A rule-~~based~~ Breaking counting book

Written by
R. A. Stephens

Illustrated by
Carmen Dougherty

To all the inquisitive
minds who ask, "Why?"

-RS & CD-

Apples Not Orples

Text © R. A. Stephens, 2024
Illustrations by Carmen Dougherty

Print ISBN: 978-1-76111-169-3

Published by Wombat Books, 2024
PO Box 302,
Chinchilla QLD 4413
Australia
www.wombatrhiza.com.au

A catalogue record for this
book is available from the
National Library of Australia

Here are **4 BOOKS.**

Here are **3** more **BOOKS.**

Let's count them!

Wow! That's 7 BOOKS.

4 + 3 = 7

Here are 2 TREES.

And another
3 TREES.

1 2 3 4 5

How many TREES are there?

2 + 3 = 5

Hey, look at that! There are 5 TREES.

Here are **3 BIKES**

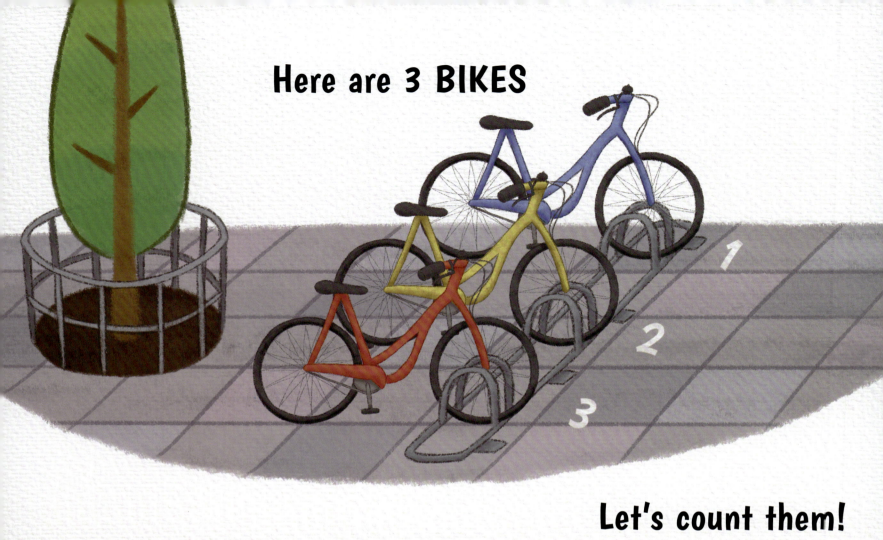

Let's count them!

and there are **4 SCOOTERS.**

NOoooOOOo!

BIKES and SCOOTERS
don't mix!

3

We just have **3 BIKES** and **4 SCOOTERS!**

4

NO!

There's no such thing as a **CHABLE!**

Where would you even sit?

I don't know.

There are 1, 2, 3, 4, 5, 6 CHAIRS! And 1 TABLE!

Ok, how about this:

5 TOMATOES
2 CARROTS
3 CARROTS

Tomato flavoured Carrots?

That sounds GROSS!

How many
CARROTS
are there?

1 2 3 4 5

How many
TOMATOES
are there?

1 2 5 4 3

Up there we have 6 TVs and down here we have 3 TVs.

What do we have all together?

6

+

3

=

9

Let's check.

Are these all the same?

YES!

So that makes 9 TVs in total.

Let's try a harder one. Ready?

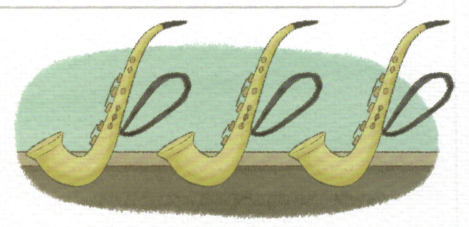

3 SAXOPHONES,

5 CELLOS,

and 2 DRUM KITS.

And on this page there are ...

2 CELLOS,

2 SAXOPHONES,

and 5 DRUM KITS.

5 CELLOS + 2 CELLOS = 7 CELLOS

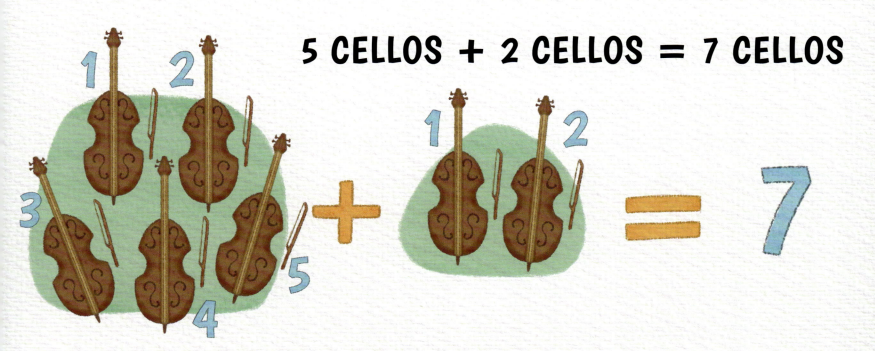

3 SAXOPHONES + 2 SAXOPHONES = 5 SAXOPHONES

2 DRUM KITS + 5 DRUM KITS = 7 DRUM KITS

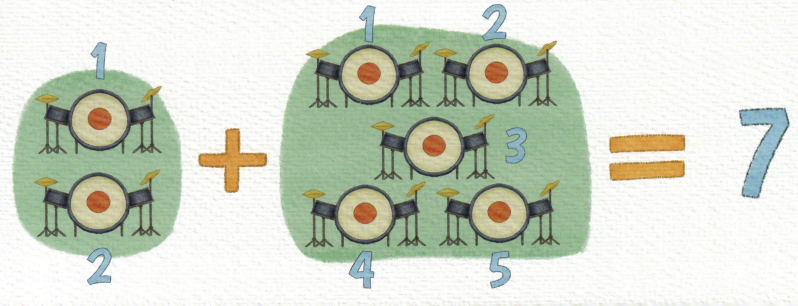

So do APPLES = ORANGES?

NO!

And they don't equal ORPLES either!

No more breaking maths!

An Apple is not an Orange!

We just covered the mathematical concept of like terms! Here are some extra clues.

In algebra we can only add letters or symbols that are the same as each other. Just like we can't mix apples and oranges to make orples!

For example $3a + 2a = 5a$

But $3a + 2o \neq 5ao$

Because the a and o are not the same. And neither are apples and oranges!

A NOTE FOR PARENTS: Understanding like terms comes up again in high school.

We can only match values that are same!